What's the Score?
and Five Other Dramas
for Tweens

Abingdon Press
Nashville

What's the Score?
and Five Other Dramas for Tweens

0-687-06597-6

Written by Nate Lee

Cover design by Vicki Williamson

04 05 06 07 08 09 10 11 12 13 - 10 9 8 7 6 5 4 3 2 1

Manufactured in the United States of America

Contents

Foretold: The Palm Sunday Story

Production Notes

Scene One requires the figures of a donkey and a colt (the foal of a donkey). You will want them either to be portable or to have ropes for the owner to hand to the disciples so that the disciples can pretend to be pulling them. (Options for making a donkey and a colt are in the Props section.) Scene Two takes place along the road with the cast having Bible-times cloaks and/or palm fronds. This drama is based on Matthew 21:1-11.

Characters

Speaking Roles:

First Disciple
Second Disciple
Donkey Owner
Littlest Child
Oldest/Biggest Person
Oldest Girl
Old Man

Secondary Roles:

Any number of people
    for entry procession
Person to carry sign (can
    double as person in the
    crowd)

Props

Scene One—donkey and colt (either a backdrop painting of the animals; or two saw horses—put on wheels or skateboard for mobility—that have sticks for necks and paper bags stuffed, painted, and attached to front for heads; or "stick donkeys" like the old-fashioned stick horses that children ride); a removable Bible-times cloak for each of the two disciples.
Scene Two—posterboard and marker to make sign that says "Later that day," Bible-times cloaks, palm fronds.

Scene One: Bethphage, at the Mount of Olives

Two of Jesus' disciples have been sent into the village. They are to follow exact instructions on finding a donkey and a colt.

Two disciples enter, obviously looking for something.

First Disciple: I don't know. Why did the Lord send us to find a donkey?

Second Disciple: A donkey and a colt, remember?

First Disciple: Yeah! Why does he need both anyway? He can't ride them both into Jerusalem.

Second Disciple: *(exasperated)* He's fulfilling the prophecy! Don't you get it? He can't just walk into Jerusalem. Zechariah foretold it: "Tell the daughter of Zion, Look, your king is coming to you, humble, and mounted on a donkey, and on a colt, the foal of a donkey." Get it?

First Disciple: Whoa! That's amazing! Here, we've been disciples all this time, and I didn't know all this stuff was foretold!

Second Disciple: Look! There's a donkey and a colt, just as Jesus said.

First Disciple: What? We're just going to walk right up and take them?

The two disciples approach the owner who is brushing down the animals or working near them.

Second Disciple: Excuse me, sir. Those are very fine animals! Are they yours?

Owner: Why, thank you. Yes, they are!

Second Disciple: The Lord needs them.

Owner: Okay. Here you go!

Second Disciple: Thank you, sir. God bless you!

The two disciples begin to walk away with the donkey and the colt.

First Disciple: That was easy.

Second Disciple: Yep! Sure was!

First Disciple: You suppose the owner knows that Zechariah prophecy, too?

Second Disciple: I think <u>he</u> knows enough to do what the Lord tells him to do.

First Disciple: Hey! You're talking about me, aren't you? Aren't you?!!

The second disciple grabs the cloak of the first disciple and puts it on the colt.

First Disciple: Hey! What are you doing?

Second Disciple: I'm putting your cloak on the colt.

First Disciple: What about your cloak?

Second Disciple: I'm putting it on the donkey.

He takes off his cloak and puts it on the donkey.

First Disciple: Oh! *(pause)* Is that foretold, too?

Second Disciple: No. It's just a nice thing to do. Don't you want the Lord to be comfortable?

First Disciple: Here! Put mine on the donkey, too.

Second Disciple: Okay. Why?

First Disciple: The prophecy says that Jesus is going to ride the donkey. I want him to have my cloak, too.

Second Disciple: *(patting the first disciple on the back and taking the first disciple's cloak from the colt and putting it on the donkey with his cloak)* You're learning. You're learning.

Scene Two: Later that day as Jesus enters Jerusalem on a donkey

A person crosses the stage holding up a sign that says "Later that day."

A crowd of people—as many as possible—begin placing palm fronds down on the ground in front of them. Some take off their cloaks and place these on the ground also. The palm branches and cloaks make a path.

Littlest Child comes racing in.

Littlest Child: He's coming! The Lord is coming!

Everyone: *(all together)* Hosanna! Hosanna! Hosanna in the highest heaven!

Random shouts of "Hosanna" continue.

Oldest/Biggest Person: *(heard above the rest)* Hosanna to the Son of David!

Oldest Girl: Blessed is the one who comes in the name of the Lord!

Everyone: *(together)* Hosanna! Hosanna! Hosanna in the highest heaven!

The following random shouts occur amid continuing "Hosannas." (If you have a large cast, these lines can be done one each by different people; if you have a small cast, assign each cast member several of the lines.)

Shout 1: Welcome to Jerusalem, Lord!

Shout 2: Look! He's riding a donkey! Just as it was foretold!

Shout 3: Look! The donkey walked on my coat! I'll never wash that coat again!

Shout 4: I'm going to follow him.

Shout 5: Yeah. I want to see where he's going.

Shout 6: I'll bet he's going to the Temple!

Shout 7: Come on! Let's go with him!

Shout 8: You think he's going to bless the money changers and the people who sell doves?

Shout 9: I don't know about you, but I'm going to get my old blind uncle and ask Jesus to cure him.

Everyone mimes watching Jesus go by on a donkey, then crowds in to follow him.

Everyone: *(together, as they move off)* Hosanna! Hosanna! Hosanna in the highest heaven!

The Littlest Child is left behind and an old man comes up to him.

Old Man: Say, sonny! Can you tell me who that man was who rode in on that donkey?

Littlest Child: Gee, mister. That was the prophet Jesus from Nazareth in Galilee. Everybody who's anybody knows that.

Old Man: *(pondering aloud)* So, that was Jesus of Nazareth, eh? Just as it was foretold 500 years ago by Zechariah!

Littlest Child: You knew Zechariah?

Old Man: *(laughs)* No, sonny. I'm old, but I'm not that old. But what are we standing around here for? Let's go listen to this Jesus fellow. Tell you what. I'll race you to the Temple. Ready. Set. Go!

The Old Man hobbles off ahead of the Littlest Child. As he hobbles along he shouts: "Hosanna! Hosanna! Hosanna!"

Littlest Child: Hey! Wait up!

The Littlest Child scurries off after the Old Man.

notes

Where Is He? Story of the Empty Tomb

Production Notes

The setting is the empty tomb early on Easter morning. The cast is limited, but could be expanded by adding Easter music of your choice to be sung by a children's and/or youth choir. This drama is based on John 20:1-18.

Note: *This drama uses the church's traditional belief that Mary Magdalene went to the tomb on Easter morning to properly prepare Jesus' body for burial. The Book of John does not say why she went to the tomb; Luke 23:50–24:1 and Mark 16:1 state that those who went to the tomb on Easter morning went for this purpose.*

Characters

Speaking Roles:

Mary Magdalene
Peter
John
Angel One
Jesus

Non-speaking Roles:

Angel Two

Props

Tomb, represented by a bench with a couple of large white cloths lying on top of it (where Jesus' body was supposed to be); bottles of "ointment" sitting near the bench; a "clay" lamp for Mary to carry in Scene One and for Peter to carry in Scene Two; optional for Scenes Two and Three—a door.

Scene One: Mary Magdalene's prayer

Takes place at or in the empty tomb on Easter morning. Mary Magdalene has come to properly prepare Jesus' body for burial as there had been no time before the sabbath began.

Mary Magdalene is either in the tomb or off-stage.

Mary: Where is my Lord? Where is he? Where have they taken him? I've come with ointments and he is no longer here in his tomb, where Joseph laid him.

Mary comes out of the tomb onto center stage.

Mary: Where is my Lord? Where have they laid him? Someone please tell me so that I may go and get him. But who would tell me? It's not yet morning.

Walks around the stage holding the clay lamp in front of her, searching.

Mary: Hello? Are you out there? Who are you who would steal the body of our Lord? Surely not robbers, or you would have taken the linens. You are of the sort that linens of the dead mean more to you than our Lord. Hello? Is someone there?

Mary looks back to the tomb.

Mary: Of course no one is there. I must be mad. Mad with grief. How could they have done this? Could this be yet another indignity? Another crime? Could it even be the last crime done to my Rabbi? My Jesus? How could they do this?

Mary: Oh, my Lord, I only wanted to see you one more time. To anoint…to touch you. How could you… How could this happen? All of this? How could you have let them do this to you? I followed you. I was your disciple, too.

It was all supposed to be different. Didn't you promise it would be different? You didn't, did you? How could we have thought it would be different? It was supposed to be different!…somehow.

I miss you so much, Lord. I only wanted to see you one more time. How could you not be here? How could you be dead? How can I go on living? Nothing will ever be the same. How can you not lead us? How can you not stay to heal even more? teach even more? keep us together?

What's going to become of us? Oh, please, Lord. Stay with us.

Mary looks around.

Mary: Strange. It should have been light by now. It's so dark. So dark. The whole world is a tomb.

Mary looks back at the tomb. Long pause while she looks at it. She sighs and drags herself to it slowly. She pauses and then approaches the tomb slowly, pauses, then enters the tomb (or goes to the bench with the cloths).

Mary: *(screaming)* Where is my Lord? Where is he?

Scene Two: A little later on Easter morning. Mary Magdalene has arrived at Peter's house.

A frightened, sobbing Mary Magdalene runs in. She is looking behind her, trips, gets up, runs across the stage, and bangs on Peter's door.

Mary: *(banging on the door)* Peter! Wake up! Wake up, Peter!

Peter: *(sleepily, from the other side of the door)* What is it?

Mary: Get up, Peter. You must come!

Peter: *(opening the door, holding up a lamp)* Is that you, Mary?

Mary: Peter. You've got to come quickly. I was just at the Lord's tomb.

Peter: *(a bit afraid, looking around)* Come inside, Mary.

Mary: Peter. Listen to me! They've moved the stone and taken the Lord's body away.

Peter: Who? Where?

Mary: I don't know. You must come!

John: *(from inside the house/backstage)* Peter? Are you all right? Who is that?

Peter: *(to John)* It's Mary. Something's happened. We're going to the Lord's tomb.

John: I better come with you.

The three of them race back across the stage and off. After a short pause, they come back on stage, preferably from a different spot. They run up to the tomb. John is ahead of the others. He looks into the tomb, then looks around, afraid. Peter comes up to the tomb.

John: There's something inside there. It looks like linen wrappings or something.

Peter: *(going in, looking around)* Right. His burial wrappings are here. And over here is the cloth that was on the Lord's head.

John: *(going in)* Both wrappings are here? Grave robbers would have never left something that expensive behind. Do you think it was Roman soldiers?

Peter: No, they wouldn't have left anything behind, for sure.

John: I think we better be getting back.

Peter: Right. We've got to tell the others. This is very strange. What—or who—would have done this?

They start to head off. They look back for Mary, who is sitting as if in a trance beside the tomb.

John: Mary?

Peter: Aren't you coming, Mary?

Mary: *(through sobs)* No. You go on. I want to stay here for a while.

Peter: *(looking around nervously)* Okay. Uhhh...we probably should be getting back. You know...to tell the others?

Mary: Go on. I'll be all right. Go ahead.

Peter and John exit.

Mary: *(to herself)* Oh, Lord. Where have they taken you? Why would they have taken you? I must touch the place where you were laid.

While Mary is speaking the two angels slip in quietly, remove the cloths, and sit on the bench.

Mary enters the tomb, stops suddenly, and gasps.

Angel One: Woman, why are you weeping?

Mary: Someone has taken away my Lord, and I don't know where they've laid him.

While Mary is speaking, Jesus slips very quietly onto the stage and stands behind her.

Angel Two points behind Mary who turns and gasps when she sees Jesus.

Mary: *(gasps)* Who are you?

Jesus: Why are you weeping? Whom are you looking for?

Mary: Sir, if you've carried him away, tell me where you have laid him, and I will take him away.

Jesus: Mary!

Mary: Rabbouni?!?!

Jesus: Do not hold on to me, because I have not yet ascended to the Father. But go to my brothers and say to them, "I am ascending to my Father and your Father, to my God and your God."

Mary: Yes, my Lord. I will. Oh, my Lord. Yes. Right away! Yes!

Jesus exits one direction and Mary runs off the stage in the other direction.

Scene Three: Peter's house. A little later on Easter morning.

Mary enters. She is running across the stage with excitement and joy. While running she is saying to herself, "Yes. I will tell them. I will tell them." She looks back, but she doesn't stumble. She arrives at Peter's house and bangs on the door.

Mary: Peter! John!

Both Peter and John come to the door.

Peter: Mary?

Mary: I saw him! He spoke to me! At the tomb!

Peter: Who?

Mary: I saw the Lord! He told me to come tell you that I had seen him, and that he is going to ascend into heaven.

John: But the Lord wasn't there.

Mary: *(growing more excited throughout)* After you left, two angels appeared in the tomb. Then the Lord was there, I tell you. I didn't recognize him at first. He called me by name. He said my name. And then, all of a sudden, I recognized him. He said not to hold on to him because he hadn't yet ascended to our Father. That's what he said. He said to tell you: "I am ascending to my Father and your Father, to my God and your God." Those were his very words.

John and Peter look at each other.

Mary: *(almost breathless)* I must tell the others. The Lord told me to tell all of you. And you know something? The angels asked me something. Then, the Lord asked me the same thing. They asked me, "Why are you weeping?" Can you imagine that? Why am I weeping?

Peter: The Lord asked you why you were weeping? He would know why you're weeping.

Mary: No. Don't you see? As soon as he asked me, I understood. I shouldn't be weeping. I should be rejoicing! He has risen! The Lord has risen!

John: You know. I felt something when I first went into the tomb. It was like that. I know what you are saying. I must have felt that...that he had risen. Now I know that feeling was true.

Mary: We must tell all the disciples. He has risen! The Lord has risen!

All Three: The Lord has risen! We must tell them all!

At this point the three can exit, or they can come out to the audience, and tell everyone at the end of the row, who then passes it down.

All: He has risen! Hallelujah! The Lord has risen!
      He has risen! Hallelujah! The Lord has risen!

notes

What Is Your Name?
The Miracle of Pentecost

Production Notes

If you are reading this in a classroom, only speaking parts are needed. However, for presentation this drama needs as many people as possible. If you have a large enough cast, have the twelve disciples in the middle. The crowd will gather in a semicircle around them. This drama is based on Acts 2.

Characters

Speaking Roles:

Matthias
Philip
Simon the Zealot
Peter
Skeptic One
Skeptic Two
Skeptic Three

Non-speaking roles:

optional: the other eight
    disciples
other crowd members

Props

Curtain; Bible-times costumes; sound of a strong wind, which can be made using large fans or by blowing into a microphone; spotlight.

When the curtain opens, Peter, Philip, Simon the Zealot, and any other of the disciples are already sitting on the stage.

Matthias enters.

Matthias: Shalom, Philip. Happy Pentecost!

Philip: And to you, Matthias. Have you gotten used to being one of the Twelve yet?

Matthias: I don't think I could be any more thankful. It's not often one is chosen by the Lord.

Philip: On the contrary, Matthias. It's not often enough that one answers the call.

Matthias: Who are all these strangers? There must be every country in the world represented.

Simon: Over there are the Parthians, Medes, Elamites, and Mesopotamians. Right there are the Judeans, Cappadocians, Pontians, and Asians. On that side are the Phrygians, Pamphylians, Egyptians, Cyrenians, and Romans.

They all laugh.

Philip: You'll have to excuse Simon. He's not showing off. He probably knows each of them by name by now.

They all laugh.

Peter: Something tells me that we are going to learn their names before the end of the day.

Simon: Is that another one of your prophecies, Peter?

Matthias: Do you hear something?

Simon: Oh, that's old Zebedee the goat herder. He regularly brings his herd by here this time of day.

Peter: That sound isn't goats, Simon!

Sound effect of an enormous sound of wind. Everyone is "thrown" about and there is lots of yelling. Then it all stops suddenly.

Simon: Okay. So, it wasn't goats!

A spotlight should be used as "fire" to light upon those in the inner circle—the disciples.

Matthias: What's that on your head, Simon?

Philip: It's fire!

Simon: Fire? Get it off? Put it out!

Philip: It's on you, too!

All the Disciples: *(pointing to each other)* It's on you. Get it off. Help! Put it out!

These calls for help change into gibberish, or if your disciple cast members can speak other languages they should start speaking in these languages about what has happened. Several languages and/or forms of gibberish that sound like languages should be used. The principle emphasis is on Simon, Peter, Matthias, and Philip. However, as many disciples as you have should join in with their own gibberish phrases. As this is going on the crowd enters and forms a semicircle around the disciples. The disciples immediately start talking to them. On the edges of the crowd are three skeptics listening.

Note: *If the characters are speaking a foreign language, each of these languages must be different or they should use the gibberish.*

Simon: slimineee sloopsall slipsey sly smilimineel slopssloom *(repeat variations of these nonsense words or substitute words from a real language that the cast member playing Simon knows how to speak)*

Matthias: zigzox zigraks roggs roggs roggs zig jag jog rogx zogs *(repeat variations of these nonsense words or substitute a real language that the cast member playing Matthias knows how to speak)*

Philip: himmm neee hee nee heee himm nam ham nee hee *(repeat variations of these nonsense words or substitute words from a real language that the cast member playing Philip knows how to speak)*

Peter: Praise be to God. Alabado sea el Señor. Ha-na-nim-eul Chan-yang-ha-ra. *(repeat)*

Skeptic One: What's wrong with these people? Aren't they from Galilee?

Skeptic Two: Yes, they are. Yet they're speaking all this gibberish.

Skeptic One: But, look. Everyone seems to be understanding them. Even the Elamites!

Skeptic Two: Come to think of it, I can understand that one! *(pointing to a disciple)* They're speaking about God's powers.

Skeptic One: It's a miracle!

Skeptic Three: Miracle! Hah! They're all drunk. Every last one of them.

Peter: *(shouting above the crowd)* Excuse me! Pardon me! HEY!!!!

All speaking ceases immediately.

Peter: Thank you! Listen to me, please, men of Judea, residents of Jerusalem, and visitors alike. First of all, I would like to make one thing perfectly clear. My friends and I are not drunk. After all, it is only nine o'clock in the morning. The miracles you have just witnessed, all of you, you must know have been foretold by the prophet Joel.

Our Lord, Jesus of Nazareth, who did deeds of wonder and miracles through God, deeds that you witnessed, who with the foreknowledge of God was crucified; this same Jesus was raised from the dead, just as David foretold.

This Jesus, whom God raised up to be at his right hand, received the promise of the Holy Spirit, and has poured forth that Holy Spirit so that all of you—all of you—may see it, may feel it, may let it be poured into you.

Skeptics: How? Please, tell us how? What do we do?

Peter: Repent, and be baptized every one of you in the name of Jesus Christ. Let your sins be forgiven. Then you will receive the gift of the Holy Spirit.

As Peter speaks the crowd gradually spreads across the stage, all facing Peter. All then gradually kneel and bow their heads. The three skeptics also kneel and bow their heads.

Peter goes to Skeptic One; then slowly Philip, then Simon, then Matthias, then each of the other disciples go over to people kneeling in the crowd.

Peter: *(loud)* What is your name? *(Skeptic One mumbles a name)* I baptize you in the name of God the Father, his Son Jesus Christ, and the Holy Spirit.

Philip: What is your name?

Simon: What is your name?

Matthias: What is your name?

Peter: What is your name?

Philip: I baptize you...

Simon: I baptize you...

Matthias: I baptize you...

Peter and All the Disciples: I baptize you...

All: ...in the name of God the Father, his Son Jesus Christ, and the Holy Spirit.

The disciples continue to go to people in the crowd as Peter addresses the audience.

Peter: On that first day, the day of Pentecost, known as the day of First Fruits, three thousand welcomed the message and were baptized. And to that first harvest, day by day the Lord adds those who would be saved. What is your name?

Peter returns to baptizing and as lights fade, "What is your name?" is heard repeated steadily.

notes

What's the Score?

Production Notes

This contemporary drama is based on a very real story of how one group of preteen girls and their parents changed a soccer league. One church standing alone made a difference. The situation was a girls' soccer team, but for presentation purposes you could use either girls' or boys' teams. The audience should be informed of the factual basis for the story.

This drama can accommodate almost any cast size. For a large cast, have large numbers of team members, parents, and coaches attending the meeting. For a small cast, you could adjust the number of speaking parts by combining some.

Characters

Speaking Roles:

Narrator/Sports Announcer
Two players from Saints
   soccer team
Four opposing team
   members (OTM)
League Commissioner
Opposing team coach
Father
Mother
Referee

Non-speaking Roles:

coach of Saints soccer team
optional: members of other
   teams, coaches, and
   parents

Props

Scene One—soccer ball, whistle for Referee, microphone for the Narrator/Sports Announcer; Scene Two—table and gavel for the League Commissioner, chairs.

Scene One: Soccer Field

The opposing team members are standing around, talking, and playing with a soccer ball. In front of them is a Sports Announcer.

Narrator/Sports Announcer: Good morning, ladies and gentlemen. What a bright and beautiful early Sunday morning. A perfect day for soccer. Well, I take that back. Some people would say it's a lousy day for soccer. Anyway, we're going to go live to our story.

Opposing Team Member (OTM) #1: You think they'll show up?

OTM #2: No way.

OTM #3: Of course not.

OTM #4: There's still time. They'll show.

OTM #2: No way.

OTM #3: This will be the fourth Sunday in a row.

OTM #1: So, we win if they don't show up. Right?

OTM #4: Here they come. I knew they'd show.

Two players from the Saints soccer team enter.

Saint #1: Hi guys.

Saint #2: How are you doing?

OTM #4: Where is the rest of your team? The game is supposed to start in two minutes.

Saint #1: That's what we came to tell you.

Saint #2: They're not coming.

OTM #1: *(jumping around)* So, we win right? Yahoo! We win. We win!!

Everyone just stares at OTM #1.

OTM #2: Who wants to win like this? We want to play.

OTM #3: Are you guys going to just forfeit all your games?

Saint #1: It was unanimous. Our whole team decided that as long as the league is going to schedule games on Sunday morning, we're going to choose Sunday school over soccer.

OTM #4: Boy, when you guys named yourselves "the Saints," you really took it literally, huh?

Saint #2: Look. It doesn't take a saint to stand up for what you believe in. We're tired of being forced to choose between soccer and church.

OTM #3: What if they kick you out of the league?

Saint #1: We've got to go. We just thought we'd come tell you so you wouldn't have to wait around.

The two Saint's players start to leave, but just then the Referee runs in blowing a whistle.

Referee: Sorry I'm late, girls. So, you ready to start the game?

OTM #1: The Saints didn't show. Again!

Referee: What? Again?! No way!

Saint #1: Yes! It's true. Well, we've got to go.

Saint #2: We're running late.

Referee: What? Wait, come back here. You forfeit the game you know!

Saint #2: You do what you have to do, ref.

Referee: *(blowing whistle)* Why, this is ridiculous. It's only a few Sundays out of the year. What's wrong with you girls?

The two girls exit, waving goodbye.

Referee: You come back here. I'm reporting you to the commissioner. This has gone too far. You'll be thrown out of the league, I'm warning you...*(then, meekly because no one is listening)* I'm warning you.

The opposing team members exit out of disgust for the Referee. The Referee finally stops blowing his or her whistle, looks around, and sulks off the field.

Scene Two: Meeting Room

A meeting of the soccer league with Team Members and Parents as well as the Referee and Coaches in attendance.

Narrator/Sports Announcer: Well, folks, you could probably hear the phones ringing all the way to where you live. The referee calls the coaches who call the commissioner who calls other coaches who call the parents who call each other. Well, you get the idea. Then, after three days of phone calls, the commissioner calls a meeting. Get it? Calls? A meeting?

The Commissioner is sitting in the middle of the stage. The Saints team members, along with their Coach (and perhaps some parents), are on one side of the stage; the Referee and some parents along with the Opposing Team Members and their Coach are on the other side.

As the lights come up on the stage:

Saints Team Members: *(chanting)* It's not right. We're no fools. We don't play during Sunday school.

Repeat chant two or three times.

At the same time the Referee is blowing his or her whistle.

Commissioner: Thank you. Excuse me, ref. That includes you. *(The Referee stops.)* Now, since we have representatives from all of the teams, we can start.

Referee: It's their fault. The Saints! We had a perfectly good schedule and they went and ruined everything! You can't boycott soccer! It's un-American. I, and more than half the coaches, want them thrown out of the league!

Commissioner: Is that true?

Referee: Well, at least one other coach, and two of my assistant refs *(pause)* and a handful of parents...I think.

Opposing Team Coach: Excuse me, commissioner. As a coach I've had other girls and their parents tell me that they'd like to skip the games for Sunday school too, but the rules say I've got to kick them off the team if they miss the Sunday games.

OTM #2: I mean, sure, it's great to win a game, but you want the other team to at least show up. Who wants to win by forfeit?

Commissioner: I see.

Father: I, for one, wish I had the guts to do what these girls and their parents did. Way to go, Saints!

Mother: Me, too. I told my husband I wanted to skip the Sunday games. He just shook his head and said *(imitating her husband)* "We're paying for soccer. And we aren't paying for Sunday school."

OTM #4: *(trying to shout over the laughter)* I'd like to say something. Excuse me!

The Referee blows the whistle. All noise stops.

OTM #4: I never wanted to go to Sunday school before. But some of my friends are on the Saints, and they love soccer and they're great players. And, well, if they choose Sunday school over soccer, there must be something to it. So, as they say in the song, *(sings to the tune of "When the Saints Go Marching In)* "I wanna be in that number, when the Saints go to Sunday school."

As she or he sings, OTM #4 crosses to the other side and joins the Saints.

Other Opposing Team Members get up and, singing, go over to join the Saints.

Various OTMs: Yeah! / Me too! / Count me in!

Various OTMs: *(singing)* Oh, when the Saints
go to Sunday school
Oh when the Saints
go to Sunday school.
I want to be in that number . . .

The Referee and maybe only one or two others are left on the other side as all the Saints and others are singing. They are interrupted by the Commissioner—still seated at the table—pounding his gavel.

Commissioner: Order! Order! Please, let's not turn this into a revival meeting just yet. After three days and three nights of phone calls, I have reviewed this matter very closely. As of tomorrow night, there will be a new schedule for girls' soccer games to be held on Saturday, and Sunday *(short pause)* afternoons. This meeting is adjourned. *(Commissioner bangs gavel in final dismissal.)*

All cast members shout with joy, and start singing "When the Saints Go Marching In."

Narrator/Sports Announcer: Well, ladies and gentlemen, there you have it. A true story of courage, sacrifice, and standing up for your beliefs, no matter what. No more Sunday morning soccer games—in this town, anyway. And even though the Saints are at the bottom of the standings, with zero wins and four straight losses, I think you'll have to agree, that right now, they all look like champions. This is Smilin' *{actor's real name}* with another true story. Now if you'll excuse me...

Announcer joins rest of cast as they all exit, singing.

notes

A Gathering of Disciples: New Testament Letter Writers

Production Notes

This is a Bible-times setting. In the drama Paul and others who wrote New Testament letters are discussing how to encourage and educate new churches. While it is not based on a specific Bible story, the drama introduces the essence of why the New Testament letters were written and read.

This play is not as flexible as others in the number of cast members. Only certain people have New Testament letters attributed to their names. However, you could have some extra disciples sitting around listening to the discussion.

Characters

Speaking Roles:

John
Peter
James
Paul
Jude

Non-speaking Roles

optional: other disciples

Props

Traditional Bible-times costumes; a "letter" in an envelope; a door (optional).

Paul is off stage. John is standing. Peter and James are seated together, with Jude off to the side a little. They are laughing at a story Peter is telling as the scene begins.

Peter: ...and then he said, "Oh, I'm so sorry. I didn't recognize you. Can I have my money back?"

Everyone laughs at this punch line.

James: Well, Peter, I guess even you can't win them all.

Peter: Maybe not, my dear James. But I can certainly try!

They all chuckle.

Knocking heard off stage.

John: Excuse me, gentlemen. *(He goes to the door, opens it, and there is Paul.)* Paul, it's you! Come in! Come in! Praise the Lord! You're two weeks late. If it were anyone else, we would have been worried.

Paul enters.

Paul: It's good to see you, John. You're looking well.

John: You're just in time. Peter, James, and Jude are here as well.

They greet and hug each other. Paul calls them each by name.

John: You just missed another one of Peter's stories.

Paul: Such good fortune! I mean, not in missing Peter's story, but in seeing all of you. There is so much to talk about.

John: Oh, you'll forgive me for this, but I must give you this letter from Corinth. It just came for you.

Paul: Corinth?! How could this be? I just came from there! *(Takes letter from John.)* Every time I hear the word Corinth, the pain in my side flares up. *(Looks at the letter.)*

Jude: What's the news, then, Paul?

Paul: Not good, Jude. The Corinth church has all these little factions competing with each other. Each thinks it has the one, true answer and that all the others are wrong. Can you imagine?

James: Unbelievable. Have they finally stopped worshiping Roman and Greek gods and goddesses?

Paul: Barely. Some even flirt with pagan rituals. *(Reading more of the letter.)* Oh! Ohhh! *(Grabs his side.)* Oh, Lord, please give me strength.

The others show signs of concern for Paul.

Peter: Are you all right, Paul? What's the matter?

John: Here. Have something to drink.

Paul: It says here they're questioning, nay denying, the Resurrection.

Peter: God, forgive them.

John: How soon can you get back there, Paul? Surely not for another year?

Paul: I need to get back to Ephesus.

John: Ephesus! Don't get me started. All of the pastors I've trained there. Still, these false teachers weed their way in and confuse the faithful.

Paul: False teachers! Don't get me started. They're the worst. Evil beasts who prey upon our sheep. They're absolutely the worst.

Peter: I agree. Church leaders who permit anything, as long as the sinners pay them. And some of them are the worst sinners of all.

John: We think we've left them with an understanding of Jesus. A true understanding. Then, as soon as we've left town...

Paul: Surely, it's not the same with you, James? I hear all over the world of your converting Jews to Christianity.

James: They're all too human too, I'm afraid. Many just mouth the words but don't do anything to back it up. I'm ashamed of all the rich Christians there are who couldn't care less about the poor.

Peter: And even though they're all Christians, the Gentiles and Jews insist on looking at their petty differences and blowing them all out of proportion.

Paul: Speaking of which, I think I solved the problem about the Galatians insisting that the Gentiles be circumcised before they can become Christians.

John: Actually, Paul, I'm afraid the reports are otherwise.

Paul: *(laying his head in his hands)* Lord, give me strength. Please tell me how I can be everywhere at all times, tending to the churches I've built while still building more. Staying alive. Staying out of prison...

Peter: Settling petty differences...

John: Trying to halt the backsliding…

James: Making sure they follow words with deeds…

Paul: Keeping out the false prophets…

Paul: *(shaking the letter)* Keeping churches from fighting each other. From saying they're the only ones with the right answer. Lord, I put it in your hands.

John: That's it. That's it!!! Oh, joy. Oh, thank you, Lord. That's it. Oh, praise the Lord. Oh, thank you. Oh, joy. Joy. Joy!

All: What? What?

John: You have opened my eyes once again, Lord. There is hope!

Peter: John, would you do us the favor of telling us? Then we can all praise the Lord!

John: The answer to being in all places at once? It's in his hands!

James: Whose? The Lord's? Or Paul's?

John: Both! Don't you see?!

Paul: You're being purposely obscure again, John.

John: I'm sorry. The letter. Paul, the way for you to reach all of God's kingdom is to write letters. Write to all these churches! Maybe Gaius or Timothy can personally carry them for you, so the churches know they're from you!

Peter: John is right, Paul. All of the churches will obey you. They will do what you say—even if you're not there—if you write to them.

John: Not just Paul. You too, Peter. The world needs to hear from Simon Peter, too. And, of course, from James and Jude.

James: You're the writer, John. What about you?

John: Oh, you can count on me, too.

Paul: *(pondering)* Letters! That's good! Yes! That gives me hope. My side feels better all ready.

Peter: I don't know what we'd do without your little revelations, John.

John: No, no. They're not my revelations, Peter. They're God's.

Peter: Amen to that.

All: Amen!

Lights fade out.

Paul: Now let me tell you a story!

All: *(random)* Oh, yes! Yes! Why were you so late? What is it with those Galatians?

notes

What About Dinner? Jesus Feeds the Five Thousand

Production Notes

This is one of the most well-known of Jesus' miracles. This drama is based on Matthew 14:13-21.

This drama can accommodate almost any cast size. For a large cast, have large numbers of disciples and people in the crowd.

Characters

Speaking Roles:

Philip
Andrew
Thomas
Jesus

Non-speaking Roles:

optional: person to carry sign
optional: other disciples
people in the crowd

Props

Baskets; five loaves of bread; two fish; posterboard and marker to make sign that says "Later that evening."

Note: The bread and the fish can be represented by pictures of these objects if the real thing is not available.

Jesus is upstage with his back mostly toward the audience, teaching the crowd massed around him. Philip and Andrew come up to Thomas, who is sitting, asleep, in the foreground.

Philip: Look. Thomas has fallen asleep. *(they nudge him)* Wake up, Thomas.

Andrew: We should be leaving soon.

Thomas: Leaving? I doubt it. Jesus has been teaching and healing non-stop since sunrise. I thought we were going to leave two hours ago. Humph! We were supposed to come here to get some rest.

Philip: You are getting rest, Thomas.

Andrew: What about dinner? We should tell Jesus to send the people away so they can go home and eat.

Thomas: Yeah. That's a good idea. *(mildly sarcastic)* You tell him that.

Philip: Alright, we will. Come on, Andrew.

They go up and pull Jesus aside from the crowd to talk to him. Thomas lazily watches from where he sits. Philip and Andrew gesture to Jesus about the crowd. Jesus calmly points to Philip and Andrew who mime "Us?" and "With what?" Jesus calmly and very quietly says something to them.

Philip: Jesus?

Jesus: Yes, Philip?

Philip: *(meekly)* Excuse me for interrupting and all, but uh...shouldn't we...uh...isn't it about time to wrap things up here?

Jesus: Why do you say that, Philip?

Philip: It's getting late. These people are probably hungry and they'll need to travel quite a ways to get something to eat.

Jesus: Why don't you feed them?

Philip: Jesus, even if we had enough money, where is there any place within miles to buy enough bread for all these people?

Jesus: How many loaves do you have?

Philip: But, Jesus...but...

Jesus: *(calmly)* Why don't you and Andrew and Thomas go see?

Andrew: We will, Jesus. We'll find bread. *(Nudges Philip who is gaping at Jesus.)*

Philip and Andrew come back to Thomas.

Thomas: *(humorously)* So, we're going now, are we?

Philip: He wants us to feed the crowd. You, too.

Thomas: Us? With what?

Philip: That's what we said. He said to go find out.

Thomas: That's crazy.

Andrew: You tell him that. We're going to look for bread.

They look around the stage, back stage, and at the audience, asking members of the audience if they have any bread. Finally, from the back of the theater, Andrew calls out.

Andrew: Hey, I found some. *(He quickly returns to the stage.)* Five loaves of bread and two fish. *(He runs up to Jesus carrying a basket.)*

Thomas: *(to Philip)* Are you thinking what I'm thinking?

Jesus: Very good, Andrew. Now have everybody sit down, please.

(Andrew, Thomas, and Philip go through the crowd—including the audience—and tell them to sit down with lines like: "Come on, now. Sit down or you won't get anything to eat.")

Jesus: *(raising bread and fish up to heaven)* Heavenly Father, we thank you for this bounty and for all your gifts. Please bless this bread and this fish and those who are about to partake of it. Amen.

All: Amen!

Jesus: Andrew, Philip, Thomas, would you please give these people the food?

Jesus gives a basket to each of the disciples. They begin to go through the crowd.

Lights fade—all leave the stage. Lights come back up. A person enters and crosses the stage carrying a sign that says "Later that evening."

Philip and Thomas enter and collapse in an exhausted heap in the middle of the stage.

Philip: So, you think they're done eating, Thomas?

Thomas: I doubt it.

Philip: Are you sure there were only five loaves of bread and two fish in that basket?

Thomas: Now that's one thing I am sure of.

Philip: How do you suppose he did it? I mean, we sat the loaves in front of each group, and they kept eating and eating and there was always more bread and fish waiting for them. Do you suppose they just took little tiny bites?

Thomas: I doubt it. They looked pretty hungry. In fact, at first I thought they were going to fight over the pieces. Then I thought that the presence of Jesus kept them from fighting. Jesus was able to feed them all with five loaves and two fish.

Philip: Feed five thousand?

Thomas: Five thousand? That was just the men. There were probably several thousand more women and children. I wouldn't have believed it if I hadn't seen it with my own eyes.

Andrew: *(entering and rushing up to Philip and Thomas)* You won't believe this. After everyone finished eating, Jesus asked us to pick up the leftover scraps. There are twelve huge baskets full of leftovers. Come see!

Philip: I've got to see this. *(getting up and running off after Andrew)* Come on, Thomas!

Thomas: *(getting up)* Now this I've got to see! Twelve baskets. Hah! *(He exits.)*

notes